VERGE 2012

INVERSE

VERGE 2012

INVERSE

EDITED BY

SAMANTHA CLIFFORD
ROSALIND MCFARLANE

MONASH University
Publishing

Monash University Publishing
Building 4, Monash University
Clayton, Victoria 3800, Australia
www.publishing.monash.edu

Monash University Publishing brings to the world publications which advance the best traditions of humane and enlightened thought.

Monash University Publishing titles pass through a rigorous process of independent peer review.

National Library of Australia Cataloguing-in-Publication entry:

Title: Verge 2012 : inverse / Samantha Clifford and Rosalind McFarlane (editors).

ISBN: 9781921867521 (pbk.)

Subjects: Creative writing--Fiction; Short stories, Australian; Short stories, English; Poetry--21st century; Poetry, Modern--21st century.

Other Authors/Contributors: Clifford, Samantha; McFarlane, Rosalind (eds). Beilharz, Amber; Dane, Ineke; Dawncy, Peter; Donaldson, Peter; Eckhaus, Camille; Hetherington, Matt; Hodge, Siobhan; Johnson, Jeremy; Luong, Jenny; Milner, Etosha; Mutard, Bruce; McNamara, Emily; Nicholls-Diver, Amy; Noske, Catherine; Rajan, Vidya; Robertson, Samuel; Stanford, Susan; Stanton, Sarah; Tan, Elizabeth; Yap, Stephanie.

Dewey Number: A823.0108

www.publishing.monash.edu/books/verge2012.html

Design: Les Thomas

Cover design: Emily McNamara

Cover images: front and back cover images by Emily McNamara.
Inside front cover image: 'Desert Bloom' by Stephanie Yap.
Inside back cover image: 'Inverse' by Jenny Luong.

Printed in Australia by Griffin Press an Accredited ISO AS/NZS 14001:2004 Environmental Management System printer.

The paper this book is printed on is certified by the Programme for the Endorsement of Forest Certification scheme. Griffin Press holds PEFC chain of custody SGS - PEFC/COC-0594. PEFC promotes environmentally responsible, socially beneficial and economically viable management of the world's forests.

CONTENTS

EDITORS' ADDRESS

Samantha Clifford
and Rosalind McFarlane

Samantha: The theme of this edition of *Verge* was conceived over coffee, as we attempted to capture the concept that would inform the journal in its eighth year. We wanted a theme that would be concerned with boundaries and what lay beyond them, of both oppositions and parallels, of writing that sought out fresh perspectives and new places to begin from. We followed this road a little way and it lead us to the idea of the 'inverse'.

Verge has undergone something of a new beginning in 2012, and for the first time the work of Monash University writers and poets features amongst works from their contemporaries in the wider Australian literary community. We hoped to reflect the depth of talent of young and emerging writers and artists, both in Melbourne and beyond, by bringing together many different forms and genres in a single collection. The resulting publication is one of our most diverse yet, featuring works of illustration, photography, comic and other visual arts together with poetry and short fiction, all inspired by our theme of 'inverse'.

Rosalind: One of the first things I was shown as a new Monash student in 2011 was a flyer for *Verge*. I also have come across borders, having done my undergraduate degree in Western Australia, and while there are many publishing opportunities there, I hadn't before seen a space deliberately set aside for creative writing by university students. I thought it was brilliant. If this were a short story I would probably put a montage here: something about growing up in an isolated area before moving to a central metropolis and all the opportunities that entails. If I wanted to follow a few clichés the tale would end with drug addiction and a realisation of the 'good old small town values' I had left behind. You will no doubt be relieved to know this is not a short story, I am not on drugs and I think the above outline would make, frankly, a terrible narrative.

S: So it is with our own (brief) narratives that this year's edition begins. When I encountered *Verge* as a second-year Arts student back in 2006, I was far from surefooted with my own writing. I didn't send any work in for consideration, thinking it sure to be rejected – a fate I did not care to suffer at the time. I see this now as something of a missed opportunity. *Verge*, at its core, was created to support this very kind of emerging (and often self-doubting) writer – to give them some space on a page, an opportunity to show what they could do. Testament to this same strength and support of both the Creative Writing Program at Monash and its champion Chandani Lokuge, was that I found myself approaching *Verge* again after all this time – as a post-graduate, as an editor, and most importantly as a proud writer myself.

Certainly, I was caught by surprise by the experience and pace of *Verge* this year. Returning home after almost a year abroad in Latin America, my mind (and heart) was still somewhere on the Bolivian antiplano, or trying to decide whether to spend my last few dollars in Buenos Aires on an edition of Borges' poetry or another bottle of Malbec. It was time to come back to reality. Our deadlines for the journal were scarily tight: we needed a fully refereed journal in just over two months, which included all of our time for submissions to be open. Ros and I quickly became familiar email pen-pals as we rallied to read, revise, referee-ready and re-edit sumissions late into the night. We reached out to friends, colleagues, fellow students and old professors, all in the name of getting the best possible version of *Verge* to publication.

R: As Sam and I discussed *Verge* with writers and artists across Australia we were continually asked about our theme, 'inverse'. For me, one of the most interesting ideas about the theme we chose this year is that it not only implies an opposite, but a particular kind of opposite. Much the same as looking in the mirror, the inverse is all the more interesting because it combines the qualities of the similar and the different. It can be both subtle and radical, consciously constructed or unknowingly present. To examine the inverse may include the unexpected or the very negation of expectations themselves. The form the inverse tends to take, however, necessitates interacting with its opposite, its other side. It is these interactions, in all their forms, which are the impetus of this year's collection.

S: Approaching our theme from a different angle, we can consider works 'In Verse', alluding to not only the poetic form but the act of writing itself. Considering *'vers'* from the Latin, a line of writing. We see a poem echo across a fading mind, bringing with it the ache of the past and those lost to it. The man who has lost his own story struggles to write another in an unfamiliar city.

R: Here 'inverse' also explores the unfamiliar self: longing not as a personal experience but a second-hand phenomenon, constant tragedy as a familiar comfort. The self is also given a different perspective: a bird's-eye view becomes the world, eating is transformed into a tradition of forgetting and fists are made of bitumen. In creating this edition of *Verge* we invite you to step through the reflection with us, to discover bruises made into mountains, vines that climb boys and the green world sloping cleanly over.

A DAY IN THE LIFE OF AN UNFORTUNATE BOY

Peter Dawncy

The unmindful mother

A boy awakes to find a creeper climbing his legs, tangling its leafy shoots about his waist up his body and attaching to his ears. He heads into a kitchen where a mother sits at a dining table.

'Don't terrify your mother like that!' the mother shrieks as she jumps to her feet. 'Get down this instant.'

The boy picks a biscuit from a biscuit tin and pours a glass of milk. 'But I'm not climbing anything,' he replies.

The mother takes a tentative step forward. 'That tree is not safe – those branches will snap!' she cries, and extends a quivering hand.

'I'm not climbing a tree though,' replies the boy, 'this creeper thing's climbing me.'

The mother takes a few more tentative steps forward. 'I won't have you climbing to such heights!' she yells, 'and I won't ask you again. Get down this instant!'

'I told you,' replies the boy, his brows narrowing, 'I'm not climbing a tree – this creeper's climbing me.'

And with that the boy starts stripping the creeper from his body.

The mother screams. 'Grab onto something! Grab on!' she cries. 'Your father's out and I can't catch you!'

But the boy just continues to strip the creeper from his body in a whirl of leaves and shredded stalks, and when at last he has torn off the final twisted tendril and thrown it to the ground, the boy returns to eating the biscuit and drinking the milk.

The mother drops to her knees and weeps. 'What shall the world think,' she wails, 'of this unmindful mother who let her child climb so high?'

The dispersion of the future

A boy is walking through a park with a mother when suddenly the mother heaves the boy into her arms.

'Ahh,' the mother sighs, twisting the boy about. 'So beautiful and delicate,' she says, 'and so ready for the dispersion of the future.'

'What?' croaks the boy.

'How have you formed so delicately?' whispers the mother as she tickles the boy's neck and then taps his forehead. 'So nuanced, and so clever. I shall never know how you've done it – only what to do with you.'

Then the mother blows on the boy's nose, and when the boy sneezes his head disappears onto the breeze in a hundred little pieces. The mother sighs.

The aged son

One night a boy walks into a kitchen where a mother and a father sit at a dining table.

'I feel strange,' the boy says to the mother and father. 'My tummy feels really bubbly and I've got pins and needles all over.'

The mother and father look to one another.

'Quick,' says the father, 'let's get dinner on before he gets too old.'

'At last!' cries the mother as she and the father head into the kitchen. 'Will he be better with lamb or beef do you think?' she asks.

'Beef,' replies the father. 'Let's get it on quickly though.'

'I thought the day would never come!' says the mother as she drops a wad of asparagus into a saucepan full of water.

'Yes,' replies the father. 'But let's get dinner on quickly.'

When the mother and father have prepared dinner and set it on the dining table, the father fetches two glasses and pours the boy into the glasses.

'This is so exciting,' says the mother. 'The day has finally arrived. But now that it's here I'm not sure how I should go about doing this – my excitement wants me to glug, but I feel that I should be sipping to savour!'

'Drink at a moderate pace,' replies the father, 'that's the sensible thing to do. He's too precious to glug, but he's also too precious for us to sip too slowly and risk him getting any older.'

JOURNEY

Vidya Rajan

Lord Shiva gets down, at a country town,
maybe named --- worth.

You spot him
at the bus stop. He's wearing a life jacket
and the remains of a tatty suit, cut at the knees.
His skin wrap is dense blue, almost
cobalt. But not a hue you've ever seen
at the beach. He stares at the traffic light
for an hour.

   Rogue electricity
does not confuse him. He wanders onto a peak hour playground
and conquers; rhyming along with the jump rope
like a pro
       pro
         pro pro .
He never discovers fists of bitumen
like you do.

But a country song
(with an early hook)
drifts across the pub floor. You both
find the other
in good spirit; the light is soft, low
and the bartender's a dear.
By midnight all the fields
are pelagic.

Ink thick in the moonlight they rise to meet
your cheery breath.

Lord Shiva dives in! -
like a prayer.
The scent of sleeping cattle -
is a prayer.
A lamb bleats
a goddamn prayer;
you follow.

Later, in the distance
you rope him into a meal
of rough potato
hospitality.
He sits gingerly
on the edge of his chair.
You point at the sky,
and proclaim the day
rightfully beautiful.

Lord Shiva asks for ice in his tea.
His blue lips dancing
a smile
against the cup rim.

Dusting the Orchid

Ineke Dane

IN VERSE

Catherine Noske

But what holds us from believing,
(given how we're set down here and placed)

I no longer know how old I am. I am old, that I know. But not *how* old –
time has slipped away from me somehow, it slides and melts away into the
cracks in the walls, the lines in my bedspread, it dissolves into a material
constancy. I think I am living in a different dimension. Everything melts
here – my hands, my face; my legs have blossomed into oedemic tubers,
delicate and painful and blue-veined. Thoughts melt, too. They run one
into another. There is a poem moving round and round inside my head,
slowly, as the time moves. I don't want it to melt away. So much, so much
melts away.

I am living my life out in vignettes of verse; only I'm never aware I am living
one until the moment has passed.

that only for a short time rage and hate
and this bewilderment linger in us,

just as once in this ornate sarcophagus

My husband came to me – yesterday, I think. He has been dead ten years
now, I know, but there he was. He wore his shirt unbuttoned, as he did
before we were married, and no old-man's vest underneath. I smiled to see
him, how I smiled! My fingers were fine-bone-china-fragile, lost in his. He
shuffled uncomfortably, plucking at one sleeve, and asked, *Why haven't you
ironed this?* I never was sure he loved me, but perhaps he did, if he felt the
need to come back. Maybe not. There is evidence for and against. I have
given up trying to decide.

Once upon a time I learnt German for Rilke. A poet makes a wonderful lover. *Eins, zwei, drei, vier, fünf, sechs.* I didn't get very far. I learnt the Lord's prayer. *Vater unser im Himmel, geheiligt werde dein Name. Sieben, acht, neun, zehn.* Now, I can't remember if I believe in God or not. In German, Rilke sounded both more beautiful and more terrible at the same time.

There are days when I feel like I could get up; just swing my legs over the side of this bed and walk out of here. My body fizzes with it. And I go, I do, I try to go – I swear it. But I never move. Because I know when I do that it won't work like that, it will never happen, my body will fold and crumple, and besides, sometimes the dream is enough.

Other times I am afraid to go to sleep. The voices that meet me there sound like Rilke in German.

...in this ornate sarcophagus
among rings, ikons, glasses, ribbons
in slowly self-consuming robes, there lay
something...

This morning I am being slowly decomposed. My skin is liquefying, my limbs expanding into gelatinous bags of melted bone. The whites of my eyes are becoming transparent, my eyeballs losing shape. They are sagging in their sockets, lumps of softened lard. The nurse this morning had to lift my body for me. I felt wet-paper-heavy in her arms. I am turning to water right before my very own eyes. Perhaps they are poisoning me.

There is a photo on my bedside table, I think it might be me. It sits in a crowded silver frame, a young girl in a bikini top, bronzed and slender and smiling. A cigarette is hanging from one hand. I can see her laugh at me, peep and giggle from behind the glass of water, the tissues, a crucifix on a gold chain that I do not recognise but which must be mine, my spectacles and the tiny statute a nurse left there, a Jesus with his arms spread wide. He is plastic made to look like ivory. The girl in the photo rolls her eyes at him from time to time. *Come to me*, his arms say. *Come and I will take you.* The girl smiles and smiles.

I am waiting to die. I do not want to die. I am waiting to want to die. It will happen, I know. It always happens, by the end.

until swallowed by those unknown mouths,

They are not feeding me anymore. People come, people are here with me. Sometimes they hold my hand. They are always quiet, silent even, or only whispering in strange, hushed tones. Sometimes, behind the crowd or at the back of the room, I see my husband again. He is smiling now. He is smiling and it is kind, and I would go to him if I could. I would have him hold me, hold me, rock me gently. I would be in his arms, safe from all the world, if I could. He is gone, when I look again. He has disappeared.

until swallowed by those unknown mouths,
that never speak. (Will there ever live and think
a brain, that would make use of them?)

The people have gone. There are nurses still. I am quite cheerful today.

I have always imagined, (or perhaps this is a more recent day-dream), that dying would involve a lifting, a movement up and away, outwards even. I have liked to think for a long time now that I would open up and drift apart, that my atoms would spread out and join… join everything. I think, perhaps, that such a death would be quite beautiful. I'm not so sure it is like that anymore. This little part of me, this little voice, these little visions, they are all that is left. I think perhaps dying is a melting inwards, I think maybe you move deeper and deeper until there is no further to go, until everything folds in on itself and collapses like the death of a star, a supernova.

Did you know that supernovae are the product of an implosion? When an aging star ceases producing energy from nuclear fusion – I watched a documentary with my grandson, Thomas – it suddenly collapses in on itself, implodes, a victim of its own gravitational forces. The energy released heats the remnants of the star, a shock wave of gasses and dust that to us, microscopic little us millions of billions of miles away, looks like a firework, a sudden blaze of light and colour. They are beautiful, apparently. No supernova has been recorded in the Milky Way since 1604.

It makes me happy, thinking like this. I tell the nurse and she listens to me with something like surprise smeared thinly across her features. Her eyebrows have been drawn on. She says, *Thomas is here, do you want to see him?* But I shake my head. He isn't here. He shouldn't be. He should be at school. He is a very bright little boy. She goes off anyway, and when she comes back there is a lumbering great hulk of a boy with her – fat, a fat slob. I don't recognise him but he cries when I ask him to leave.

When we watched the documentary about supernovae, Thomas ate golden syrup and butter on bread and sat at the foot of my chair. Occasionally, just occasionally, I let myself reach down to stroke his head. I didn't want him to think his Grandma was a sissy.

Then from the ancient aqueducts
Then from the anc...
Then from the ancient

My mother told me once that crying over a man was stupid; a silly thing to do when there were so many of them out there, better ones, different ones, ones who will love you properly. I think I might have turned to her and told her to go away, I don't remember quite, but I am sure, at least, that she never said it again. Then another time my daughter came to me and curled up in my lap and said, *don't cry, don't cry Mama* and her voice was so broken that I cried all the more.

I am connected now to tubes and tubes and tubes, and they tie me down in place. I cannot move my hands anymore. They feel cold in my veins, and my mouth is dry, but when I ask all they give me is ice, ice, tiny chips that disappear into nothingness on the dry expanse of my tongue. I want water, cool and pure and wet, I want to feel it wash me away. I am cold. Give me my ice.

She is here, my daughter. I think she is the one who is holding my hand but I am not brave enough to ask. She has grown. Lord, she has grown! She is so beautiful now.

I am so tired. I feel it melting into me, becoming part of me, stronger than real flesh or bone. I am so tired, and so in love, and that is melting inwards as well. If I am a supernova then it will be love that colours me as I go.

I am so tired.

Then from the ancient aqueducts
eternal water rushes in: –
that mirrors now and moves and sparkles
            through them.

I am so very, very tired.

Excerpts all taken from Rainer Marie Rilke, 'Roman Sarcophagi', *Neue Gedichte* (1907), translation, C.A. Noske.

VINEGAR

Elizabeth Tan

We killed the inhabitants because we were dying. We do not think our actions improper. During the famine our stomachs bloated, thickened like voices. Our hunger had depth, and it was the solemn, infinite keel of gravity itself. We killed them because we were starving.

Fattened by millennia, they grew silently under their single moon, a pocket of existence under no jurisdiction. We knew as much about them as did the other colonies, and were as disinterested as the other colonies. Their nutritional value was not scientifically confirmed, but estimated, in one obscure study, to be negligible for most species.

The famine made us desperate. We conducted our own studies. Our first attempt resulted in the destruction of the specimen. After transportation, it was unusable. Subsequent attempts were conducted in the sample's habitat. If we were to eat them, we soon realised, we would have to do so within their habitat. Our initial tests confirmed they were not poisonous.

During the famine, our technology had become rudimentary. We determined that one inhabitant was enough sustenance for just a quarter of a complete consumption cycle. Infants, almost nothing. As a source of nutrition, the inhabitants were barely sufficient, uneconomical even as a last resort. They did not have a discernible taste. But hunger has beggar's eyes. We were turned simple by it, prideless.

The harvest was completed in a single day. We would not have had the technology for a war, nor did we have the infrastructure to cultivate the inhabitants. We were willing to die if we did not succeed with just one harvest.

Our studies confirmed that the inhabitants died without pain.

We feasted for several days. We did nothing except eat. By the third day, our mental acuity was restored to pre-famine level. Our thoughts could finally return to us, and we examined the habitat, all the dead specimens. Some of them were beginning to expire or succumb to ecological feedback. We did not know how much longer we would have to endure the famine.

Now that we had eaten, we could birth the technology to preserve the inhabitants so they would not disintegrate during travel. This process took us one week. We estimated that about five per cent of the inhabitants were unrecoverable. We deemed the harvest a success.

We subsisted on the preserved specimens for three months. After that time the famine ceased. Finally, we could eat our own food again. So grateful for this miracle, and so traumatised by the memory of hunger, we created a new tradition. Once a year, we consumed some of the specimens in remembrance of the famine. We developed the technology to preserve the remaining specimens indefinitely.

We did not consider trading the specimens with other colonies because the specimens were no longer mere sustenance, but gravely significant, a part of our history.

Over time, the tradition dwindled along with the supply of specimens. Our colony saw prosperity like no other. The specimens became a delicacy, eaten in sliver and wafer. The years had finally granted them taste, or perhaps the famine had instilled us with a permanent gratitude. The vinegar is our memory.

It was not until we had only seven specimens left that another colony began to question us. We were forthcoming about the history of the specimens. We did not realise that the inquiry would persist. We reiterated that the specimens had come from an area under no jurisdiction. We gave them data about the famine. We shared our research about the specimens, but of course, with so few left, the information was nearly obsolete. We continued to consume specimens during the inquiry.

We have scanned the original habitat several times. We are certain that there are no surviving specimens.

We understand that this inquiry is neutral, a census of the world's resources and history. We do not think we have done anything improper. We are about to begin consuming the very last specimen. As an act of peace, and as the final stage of submitting our traumatic history to the archives, we have decided to divide the last specimen amongst the colonies. Each colony may do with their piece of the specimen as they wish. As for us, we have revived our tradition and will continue to eat this last specimen in exponentially smaller portions. We have the technology.

During the famine, there was a saying: *Prosperity is relative survival.* We told ourselves this as a reminder that suffering can be as arbitrary as prosperity. It was not our fault that we were starving. Sometimes there is no discernible causality, for this or any other events that circumscribe us. Perhaps that is why our trauma has remained unarticulated for the longest time. We eat silently, and silence eats us.

Our eyes, enlarged by memory, admit light; our cells are honeyed with maturity. We have persisted. We build, and build, and build.

BEGIN AGAIN

Matt Hetherington

the extent of your responsibilities
take a thing
without wincing
silently
and the colours are sharper
then with the speed of
in a nightmare, because
some mornings, you can't
and every noise you know you're not
each move
is leaden
daylight lengthening, the heart
scrapes at your temples
begins to unclog itself
and becoming clear is

ONCE, FROM UP THERE

Catherine Noske

Once, her father took her; up the mountain. It was summer, and they hiked. Up there, looking out... oh, she was just a child, then. But up there, looking out, the whole world was a tapestry of colours: gold and yellow and dun-brown, green and grey fading into the purple and blue of the hills. Her hills. That is what she thought, up there that day. The blue and purple of her hills, a mass of swollen bruises. Strange thought, for a child. But wrapped in the arms of the hills, the world was safe and warm and beautiful. Endless. Wonderful. They drank from a spring on the way down, crystal water trickling hidden from a rock, and it felt like a miracle.

She dreams about that walk. She wakes sometimes knowing she went back there in her sleep. They stopped at a pub on the way home. There were men there, three of them, friends; they drank beer with her father. They talked about football, the weather. She has no idea who the men were, but she remembers them being happy, laughing, joking. They sat outside. Her father bought Barney Banana ice-creams. Beer and Barney Bananas. They left when the sun started to go down, and she fell asleep at the table. She must, she thinks, have been quite young. Even now, though, the smell of beer can take her back there.

⁓

She thinks about it at the kitchen table that morning. She can hear the baby yowling in his cot, but she lets him be for a moment or two, lets herself sit and dream in the warmth of the watery sun. Max has gone. He whistled as he walked out the door, she thinks. She can imagine him, spinning his keys around a finger, happy, confident. She inhales slowly, tries to swallow the lump in her throat. She wonders if he noticed that she was awake when he got up. She doesn't think so. She has become quite adept at feigning sleep. The baby draws breath and his crying gathers an octave. She smiles gently. She loves her baby. He reminds her of all that is good in her world, the important things. He is easy to satisfy. His tiny hands knead at her when she feeds him, and he smells of milk and soap. She loves her baby. She stands, she stretches, and she goes to him. Smile, she thinks. A new day.

When she has fed and cleaned and dressed him, the baby is happy again. She leaves him closeted safe in his playpen, singing strings of meaningless words on the patchwork rug that once was her mother's, and shuts herself in the bathroom. The steam from the bath draws itself in artistic spirals along the length of the mirror, momentarily fades and instantly draws again. She stretches herself slowly into the water and closes her eyes. The hills, she thinks… but they are gone, they won't come back, she can't make them, and instead she forces herself to run her hands down her sides, down each arm and assess the damage. The bruises are angry reds and blues fading to a mottled yellow and green, her neck, one arm, one side, one she doesn't remember on her thigh. The water is uncomfortably hot, and she sweats gently; she can feel it beginning to bead on her forehead. She runs the cold tap and it burbles in, burbles like the baby. Sitting there, she doesn't know what to do. He will be home by six.

She gets dressed, after lunch. She puts on a dress with long sleeves and a row of buttons that march their way up from the small of her back. It makes her feel young, this dress, and she loves it. With the baby on one hip she is beautiful and light and everything she should be. She smiles. Somehow, no one expects an abused woman to wear a pretty dress. She puts lipstick on, and a touch of mascara. She straps the baby in and they drive together into the town. She talks to him as they go, tells him the colours and the names of the trees, the flowers, the animals and she is almost happy. She can't remember if the white ones are ghost gums or silver gums, but she tells herself it doesn't matter. Her father would have known. The row of poplars down the Hendersons' drive is a dirty yellow against the grey sky. Banks of clouds scud softly across above them, pregnant with rain. By the time she is driving down the main street the morning sun has disappeared into a niggling drizzle, and she is wishing she had worn something heavier than her dress. There is an oilskin in the back. It is stiff and mildewed, and it smells of the dogs, but she pulls it on like a veil over her and the baby, and giggles and coos at the look on his face as awkwardly she shuffles them into the store.

She pauses inside the door to wriggle out from under the coat. At the sound of the bell, Maggie looks up from her magazine, and bustles her wide hips over to take the baby.

'Pretty dress today, love! You got sommink planned for that man of yours?'

She smiles and flicks demure eyes up at the older lady. Play the game, she tells herself. The oilskin drips a pattern on the door mat.

'Fresh veggies, Maggie? And something for dessert... you got any fruit?'

'Tins, honey, or fresh?'

'Oh, tins will do!' She says, and tries not to mind as the older woman bounces her baby up and down, up and down on the counter.

'Down the back. I'll mind your little bundle,' Maggie says, and smiles at him with a warmth that makes her eyes crinkle. Poor lonely old girl, she thinks, and drifts off down the crooked aisle to find the tins. They are dusty, and hidden behind some forgotten packets of sweet biscuits. There is a choice of pineapple or peach, and the anxiety she has been holding off creeps up on her as she tries to decide. Pineapple. Peach? Pineapple with ice-cream. She shakes herself gently, sets her mouth.

'And how is your Max? He's a treasure, that one. And that game last week! Dunno what we'd do without 'im.' Maggie calls.

'Oh, he's fine. Working hard right now.' She calls back, automatically. Pineapple then, and she goes to find some ice-cream to go with it. The vegetables are in a wire basket up at the front, a measly selection of carrots and turnips and potatoes. She should have gone into Warrnambool, shouldn't have sat in the bath, should have made time. She finds some wilted broccoli down below, and makes up for it with plenty of the potatoes. She sighs. It will do. It's better than frozen veg, at least. It will be fine, she tells herself, and dumps it all on the counter beside her gurgling, chuckling baby. Really, she thinks, as Maggie adds it up, she must start her own veggie garden. A little one wouldn't be too hard. She swings the baby up and onto her hip without thinking, onto her bad side, and she gasps and stiffens as he kicks his feet against her bruises. She freezes, eyes wide. A fall, she thinks, it was a fall; but Maggie doesn't notice, and she breathes deep and shifts the baby to her other hip.

'Seventeen fifty, my dear.' Maggie says, piling it all into an old plastic bag.

'Put it on the tab, could you please?' She says, draping the oilskin over them again.

'Will do!' Maggie calls, as the bell jangles behind them, and she shuffles out.

She finds herself singing to the baby as she walks down the street, *we're going to have a dinner, we're going to have a dinner*, and she wonders if she is beginning to go mad. Mr. Johnson from the feed-store nods and smiles at her as she goes past, and she smiles back. The drizzle stops, suddenly, and she lets the oilskin slide off her head down onto her shoulders, feels it settle there, and tucks it in around the baby so only his face is showing. She stops and drops the plastic bag in the car, and runs a furtive hand once more down her bruises. Sissy, she tells herself, gasping like that. They aren't that bad. She wonders what colour they will be by the time she gets home. She considers dropping the oilskin too, but it is cool, not at all the sunny day she was hoping for, and she doesn't want the baby to get cold. In the end she leaves it on, draped around her like a great, leathery cape; a protective hide between herself and the sky. It feels heavy, today. The clouds are building to blue and purple. It will rain tonight, she thinks, bucket down, probably. She wonders if Max will be wet when he comes home, and if they will finish up early. She pauses in front of the coffee shop, and sniffs delicately at the smell of the beans and pastry. No, no time, better to head home and get organized, she thinks. Bread then, and off. She can stop at the butchers on the way.

She has plenty of time, in the end. The roast is in the oven and almost done by the time he comes in. He smells of sheep, and the mud has clawed its way through the grease on his hands to settle under his fingernails and in the cracks of his skin. He looks good, though, despite it all – even muddy and wet he is attractive. He always was. He spends half an hour in the shower and comes out damp and red-skinned, clean and smelling of lavender soap. She has the dinner almost ready, she is just finishing the gravy, and they eat at the kitchen table almost in silence. He is in a good mood, she thinks. He smiles and winks at her, and plays with the baby as she does the washing up. It is fine, she thinks, fine. The relief whistles through her like a drug. By the time they go to bed, she is verging on euphoric; she laughs out loud like a teenager when he takes her nighty off.

The next two days are like that. Her bruises fade, purple to green to yellow. She watches them in the bath each morning, traces the patterns they make, tries to see them as beautiful. Once upon a time, bruises were something to be proud of, something to show off. If she lets herself, sometimes she can work her way back to that, that concept. Imagine her way back into her fifteen-year-old head and peel back a t-shirt to show a bruise to a friend. Or imagine showing it, at least. Wink. How tough am I? Laugh. Ignore the little voice whispering to her, *not tough, not tough at all*. And each day the tension rises – easy day, busy day, a little anxious by lunchtime, white in the face by the time he gets home. But it is ok, she tells herself. It is normal. They are normal. When she lets herself relax she feels like she is living someone else's life.

She plans, too. Very carefully. Dinner must be good. Desert is best, he has a sweet-tooth, always has had. Everything should always be ready, in place. And tidy, too; like his mother's home. She is careful about that one. And she has her tricks. It makes her feel guilty, thinking like this, but she can't help it sometimes. Water his drinks. Wear a pretty dress. Any bad news, make sure the baby is there.

'Kippa called,' she says. 'Can't play footy this weekend.'

'Shit,' he mutters, and the baby stops bouncing in his lap. 'That's gonna hurt.' The baby gurgles, chuckles, hits him on the nose. 'Oi, tiger, you gonna play forward?' He laughs. 'Gonna come help Daddy save the day again?' She smiles. She breathes. He wouldn't hurt the child. He would never hurt a child. They can go on like this. They are happy, like this. It feels almost surreal, this life. She lets herself relax, sometimes, for days at a time. A week. Two. It slips, of course. It always does. And then she pays. But until then, until then they are happy, they are ok.

He sleeps late, the next time. Accidentally – she hit the wrong button on the alarm. He holds it in, but she can feel it there, the anger. Simmering, almost. It twists him, slightly, not so you'd notice, but just a little around the mouth. She knows that mouth, has known it as long as she has known him. Before they were married it was just a mouth, just a strange little quirk, a question mark with no question. Now she knows what it means, at least. There is something hard, tight about his face when he looks like that, and it makes the hair on her neck crawl. She starts cleaning, as soon as he is gone.

Dinner is ready by the time she hears his truck. The dogs bay at him from their chains. The house is clean, the baby clean and fed, the fire lit. It is rosy, inside, warm and comfortable; she sits waiting, her stomach tight, her fingers tying invisible knots again and again and again. He parks around the back. She catches a glimpse of him through the kitchen window, and almost cries out with relief. He is limping. Hurt. He will need her. Nothing will happen tonight. Breathe, she thinks, and reassembles her face, removes the laugh, smoothes away the tension. The back door bangs. She forces herself to get up, to rush to him and fuss, pet, worry. He is fine, a big child when hurt. She cares for him as tenderly as the baby.

It is his ankle, again, that he hurt; and they lose the football. She sees him on the bench at three-quarter time, snarling as he wraps layer on extra layer of tape around it. The baby chuckles and points.

'Daddaadadadaad,' he says, and laughs.

'Yes, darling,' she whispers, 'Dad, Dad, Dad.'

He almost clobbers the young forward replacing Kippa in the final quarter. She sees it coming and looks away. As they walk off the field, heads hung, the locals sigh and wrap their scarves a little tighter. It was a dirty game, they mutter. Coulda used Kipp. She looks around at them all and wants to cry. Why do you care? She wants to ask. Why does it matter so very, very much? She watches for him, as they come out of the showers. Men, boys, friends, burly shoulders and overweight tradies. He is last. He has been sitting there, she knows, just sitting, not talking. He looks across at her, and his face is a storm-front. Smile, she thinks, sympathetic smile; he looks away. There are no speeches, today. They all sit at the bar and drink. She can't stand it, soon. The smell, the stupidity, the depression. She leaves as soon as she thinks he will let her.

'Going to put the little one down for the night,' she says, and he nods and kisses her on the cheek. He isn't there, she thinks, and it sends a little shiver through her.

'I'll be at the pub.'

'You won't be too late?' She asks, but he just looks at her, blank, empty, and doesn't answer. She feels it coming, again, as she straps baby into his car-seat. It shivers down the back of her neck like a premonition. Tonight, she thinks. It will be tonight. She is buzzing by the time she drives out of the oval. Plan. She needs a plan. She gets home and feeds the baby, and tries to think.

'Carefully,' she says, and he smiles at her, waves his arms. He is beautiful, this little child of hers, and precious, so precious... She will give him the cough syrup. He smiles again, and she smiles back. It hurts, almost. The tension of it builds in her stomach like acid. Carefully, she thinks again, carefully; and she tries desperately to convince herself it will be fine.

He is late home. It is gone two when she hears the car, someone yelling at him, his bumbling and growling as he opens the back door. He is in the kitchen. She lies frozen, wraps the doona a little tighter, tries to pretend herself to sleep again. Please, she is thinking. Please, please. The fridge door slams. A bottle breaks, and she winces. There is a loud scraping noise, she can imagine him falling over a chair. He yells, suddenly, inarticulate almost. There is more breaking glass, and a cracking noise she can't identify. Don't wake, little one, she is thinking; and God, please, please let the cough syrup be strong enough. He is muttering again, and she feels her breathing accelerate. There are footsteps, tiles onto carpet... he is there.

'Know your 'wake,' he slurs. 'Thin' you can jus' ignore me?' And so it starts, she thinks, and bites her lip. 'Bitch, I'm talking to you,' he says, louder, and stumbles to the bed, pulls her over by one shoulder. He is bleeding from one hand. 'I'm talking to you...' She looks at him, squarely. Bastard, she is thinking. Bastard. But it is no good. It is too late. There is nothing she can do now. The questions starts, then the accusations. Gently, girl, she thinks, and keeps her eyes down. It is not that bad, in the end. Not really. It has been worse. At least she knows how to handle him, now, how to talk him around. He cries, afterwards, the violence all spent; and she holds his shaggy, great head in her lap. The tears soak through the cotton of her nighty, leave a large, round wet patch down the front. When he tries to kiss her neck, pulls at the nighty, she just closes her eyes and lets him.

She dreams that night. She is up the mountain again, but her father is not there, and it is not afternoon, there is no golden light, no sunshine and beer. It is dark, shadowy, everything below her is deep red and purple, but still she can see so far! *Higher, go higher,* her blood tells her, *go higher,* and she is scrambling, running, clawing her way up; the air is cold and free on her face. *Go higher,* but there is no higher to go, she is there, she is at the top, and all of it, her hills, all of it is spread out dark and alive beneath her. The hills are bruises. The hills are like bruises.

DEFINITIONS

Amber Beilharz

You were always taught to define
words that expand outwards: tragedy
is a silence rediscovered by lovers
and grief, a constant fever ache of visions:

you lead yourself like a herd. The field of stocky
creatures weaken their stride, their dappled calf
faces hang low as if shamed. Landscape falls,
unwittingly, their hooves hush, balmy flanks heave

and swell, breath thermal against wind.
You lead yourself to your knees, lethargic and empty
and your uncertainty: a metronome swaying
with the creature-heads to the composition of fear.

THE BLUE HAT

Camille Eckhaus

The city is concrete and cement and a cloud of sound always coming closer. As Kieran walks it beats its rhythm inside his skull. In the cold his knees crackle like old parchment. He's holding onto Tim's hand but it's just wool-wrapped skin and bone pulling him along. All he feels is the itch of the fibres against his palm. Only faintly does he remember where they're going.

Tim skids on a patch of ice and grasps at his father's arm to keep from falling. Kieran looks down at the tiny hand gripping his elbow, a shapeless thing wrapped up tight. He looks at his son's laughing face. The tips of Tim's ears are red.

Kieran has forgotten to make him wear his hat again. He can't seem to stop forgetting the hat.

He's not used to this place. It still doesn't make sense to Kieran that the cold can burn. He remembers the coat because the wind bites, the gloves because his hands claw with cold, but the hat he can't remember. Filled up with things in this strange new place, he can't seem to find space to fit everything he needs to remember. He should have remembered Tim's hat. A man walks past, shiny shoes and sleek hair, and glances at Tim. Kieran knows that man is thinking the same thing. *That man has forgotten his son's hat. Disgraceful. How could he?* Kieran feels the censure follow him down the street, a hundred pairs of eyes staring at the back of his neck.

Tim enjoys the snow. He pulls at his father's hand, the exuberance caught under his skin pushing in every direction. He wants to go everywhere, to see everything. He doesn't want to walk to school slow and holding his father's hand like a child. Kieran feels the impatience leaching out of him but says nothing. He's thinking blurred thoughts about the colour of sunshine.

He drops Tim off at school, an imposing building of red-grey cement and iron railings. All around him mothers kiss their sons, call after them to make sure they have money for lunch. All the boys have money for lunch. All the boys have hats on. A teacher is standing in the courtyard watching the children and their mothers. Her hair is grey and her clothes are the colour of red-earth mud. She looks like she's been built to match the school from spare fabric and leftover paint. She frowns when she sees Tim has no hat. This is the third time. Kieran knows that in her head she's already composing a letter to send home. He can see the words shuttle across her eyes. *Dear Mr. and Mrs. Dale* ... Before they moved here they never got those letters. Now there are two hidden in the bottom draw of Kieran's desk.

He walks home. The sky is the colour of fine dust. People push past him, their winter jackets bubbles of impenetrable space. They smell of burnt coffee and sticky-sweet perfume.

When he gets to their building the doorman holds the door for him. Kieran likes to think he and the doorman are friends. Close friends. They never speak to each other but that's because they don't have to. They just have to nod and the other understands. Today the doorman's nod is an upwards jerk of his chin, second chin following a moment behind the first. 'Hey man,' his nod says, 'shame about the hat.' Kieran nods, head dropping slightly and eyes on the carpet.

'My bad,' he is saying. '*Mea culpa*.' He passes on.

The hallway smells of fried onion, washing powder and wet paint. He breathes in and his lungs are full of the city. Thomas Wolfe breathed in this city and his lungs tore themselves apart to get it out. Kieran's are just dissolving, quiet and secret.

As he tries to open the door he fumbles the lock, gloves making his hands clumsy. He takes them off and tries again. His hands feel like they belong to someone else. When he finally gets the door open the silence sweeps out to meet him. He steps inside and takes off his coat. Hangs it on one of the pegs by the door. Tim's hat is on the peg next to it.

The apartment is cold, air hanging with ice. Kieran turns the heating on but there's no rumble of waking pipes. This building is new. Everything is efficient and streamlined. Clean and white and heavy. It's like a face of a strong chin and protruding nose. Handsome but hard. It's a face that can be admired but not loved. It can't be lived with. He hadn't wanted to live here. He'd wanted a proper house with a yard for Tim. Space for a dog. That was before he knew that everyone in this city lives in the air, not on the ground.

Jeanne has already gone to work. He can hear the echo of the noise she left behind. The click of heels and the clatter of keys. He follows her remnants through the house, finds the note she's left on the kitchen table. There is a series of x's on the front just like she used to do when they first met. When everything about them was eager and anxious. It's not something she's done in a while. The house in the suburbs and the dog and the two cars made a few x's at the bottom of a note unnecessary. The world around them was a testament to the permanence of their love. There was none of the urgency that comes with courtship, with the having before the becoming.

But now they have to become all over again. Packed up the house and given the dog to a neighbour and flown thousands of miles to a city in which the sky is full of dirt. Now Jeanne has started putting the x's back on her notes.

This city is home for Jeanne. This is the city that spawned her, raised her, taught her. This city is the mother that sent her on her way when she was old enough to go but welcomed her back when she wanted to return. When they take Tim out on the weekends she is as full of delight as he is. She shows him things that she knew as a child, places she used to go. Her excitement is like a spark under her skin, flaring brighter and brighter. She glows like the nineteen-year-old with the shaved head drinking beer through a straw, like the graduate, like the new mother. It's the shade to every memory Kieran treasures like the sepia tint to old photographs.

Kieran tries but he can't join in her excitement. His body is just too heavy. He misses the big house that was always warm and the stairs that creaked and Fitzgerald asleep at his feet, tail twitching as he dreams. He misses the sound of Jeanne's bare feet as she passed his study. He misses the voices of his friends. He wants to hear a familiar male voice, the heavy, heated vowels of an adult male.

Work has drawn Jeanne back. The job that couldn't be passed up. Fear was a living, breathing thing when Kieran's protests had tried to drag it all away from her. 'You can write anywhere,' Jeanne had said, the yellow ripple of a whine in her voice.

He hadn't argued with her because how could he explain that a writer can't just write anywhere? That he needed his study with its large windows and full bookshelves. That his job was like being wrapped in a spider web. One wrong twitch and it would all fall apart. He'd tried explaining it once, back before they got old. She'd laughed and shaken her head and said, 'Talk to me about stock trends. That I understand.'

The top three buttons of her silk blouse had been open, strips of skin melted caramel beneath, so he'd let himself be distracted. When it mattered it was too late to try again. Now they've been here for two months and he hasn't written a word.

He throws Jeanne's note away unread. He's already decided what it says.

Sweetheart. Gone to work. Re dinner: don't wait for me. Make sure Tim doesn't forget his hat. It's cold out. XXXX

Kieran decides he'll be annoyed that she's working late again, that he has to cook. He hates cooking. The part about Tim's hat he'll read as a rebuke.

He'll feel guilty about it, impotently angry. He plans a conversation in which he demands she get Tim up in the morning, dress him, take him to school. He'll demand to know why it's him who must always remember, why it's him that must be the mother. He sees himself standing in the kitchen with arms spread wide. In the conversation-dream Jeanne will stand in the doorway, arms crossed over her chest. She will be dismissive. Cruel and cold. The high ground will be irretrievably his.

He sits down at his desk. He will remember to take the hat with him when he goes to pick Tim up.

In the apartment there's no room for a study. There isn't even enough room for all his books. The meagre shelves are taken up with Jeanne's coffee-table books, spines unbroken and glossy pictures unmarked. Kieran's dog-eared books covered in scrawl are stacked in cupboards and under beds and in piles on the small table pressed tight into a corner of the living room that has become his desk. He has to fight with Vonnegut and Thoreau for elbowroom.

He sits at his desk. He picks up his pen. It feels too heavy. He puts it down and takes off his shoes. There's a hole in the toe of his left sock. He straightens the paper on his desk and picks up the pen again. Puts it down and goes to make tea. There is none, only the expensive coffee beans Jeanne buys. She says they have to be whole beans for the flavour. She says the smell is rich and chocolaty. To Kieran they smell sour. He puts them away and goes back to the desk. He stares at the blank sheet of paper. He resolves to buy tea on the way home from picking Tim up. Buy the tea and take the hat.

He writes it down. His page now says:

Tea.

Hat.

From where he's sitting he can see the hat. Blue and woollen and hanging by his coat. He thinks that today he could write about a hat. A hat that's sitting on a peg all alone in a big room. A remnant of all the people who have come and gone. A hat that still carries its wearer's scent. Or maybe he won't write about a hat but about a man writing about a hat. This man will be contemplating this hat, small enough to fit the vulnerable curve of a child's head. He will describe the hat in excruciating detail. People will read it and know every stitch. They will believe the hat is sitting there in front of them. They are not reading a story but staring at the picture of a hat. A small blue hat the colour of the sky in spring.

No. Not the sky in spring. He hasn't seen the spring sky here. It may be the wrong shade of blue. It might not be blue at all. He will have to find a new metaphor. In this place all his metaphors will have to be new. Everything he knows is the wrong way around.

Maybe instead of writing about the hat he will draw a picture. He will draw a picture and call it *The Hat* and introduce the story with the words 'This is a hat'. People will be fascinated. They will want to know what this hat means. They will write to him and ask and he won't tell them it's only a hat. It's only a hat.

Kieran gets up, goes to the bathroom, comes back. The page is blank except for:

Tea.

Hat.

Maybe instead of a man writing about a hat he will write about a man having a conversation with a hat. 'Hello,' the hat will say. 'I am a hat.' 'Hello hat,' the man says. 'Would you like to hear a story?' 'Yes,' replies the hat. 'I would very much like to hear a story.' 'Alright,' says the man. 'Here is a story. One day two men walked into a bar.' 'Was one of them wearing a hat?' the hat asks.

No, the page is almost blank (*Tea. Hat.*) and he will not write about a man talking to a hat. It seems the hat has nothing to say.

Kieran gets up and goes to the bedroom. He'd made the bed before he left but there's the shape of Jeanne where she sat to put on her shoes. He can see her do it, toes pointed as the shoe slips on, skirt riding up the stockinged thighs. He used to enjoy watching that. When she knew he was watching, she'd do it as slowly as she could.

He lies down in the centre of the bed, on his back and arms spread wide. He stares at the ceiling. It's white. There are no cracks. Kieran wants cracks. He wants to see a story he can steal pressed into the plaster. Instead he has whitewashed freshness. Anger rouses briefly then rolls over and goes back to sleep. It's too cold for anger. He turns his head. The city outside his window is huge.

He thinks about the hat. Perhaps the hat is not a hat. Perhaps the hat is the man's son. Maybe he's forgot his son. He's left his son behind somewhere. Or his son has left him. No. That won't work. Sons are always leaving fathers. That's the point of sons, of fathers. Mothers you can come back to but fathers you're always trying to leave.

Perhaps the hat is his wife. He has followed the hat, caught in the breeze. Followed the hat somewhere where the spring sky is not blue and everything is inside out. But a breeze isn't strong enough to carry a man anywhere. It can't turn him inside out. It would have to be something else.

Maybe he could be like Oliver Sachs' patient and be the man who mistook his wife for a hat. Only that won't work either. The man he writes about, that man's wife will always be a person. The kind that will fill a room with herself. She is incapable of being an object and he isn't the kind of man who can be caught in the breeze or mistake his wife for a thing. Neither is violent enough.

No, Kieran thinks, lying spread-eagled on the bed, the hat is a hat. It cannot be made into anything else.

The room smells of clean linen and smoke. Beside the bed there's a photo of the family. Jeanne put it there. He doesn't like it. He doesn't like those eyes always on him while he sleeps. It's Tim's fifth birthday in the photo. He is missing two front teeth and there is icing on his nose. Jeanne is beside him in a green sundress. Her hair is long and dark. Kieran remembers that day she'd smelt like ginger lily and cinnamon. He had wanted to touch her.

He's looking at the photo and it's looking back at him but he must have fallen to sleep because he closes his eyes and when he opens them again it's to a new shapeless world. A world that's cold and hot and loud and full of silence. He's trying to speak but can't. His own voice has become a woman's, singing a soft lullaby. He doesn't know who he's singing to. He's looking at his hands and they're covered with ink.

The clock ticks over the hour. He hears it in his dream and he knows he has to get up. He has to go back to his desk and work. He has to work and then he has to get to the school on time to pick Tim up. He has to walk through the hallway with its stiff carpet and go down in the lift that smells like steel and oil. He has to walk past the doorman so they can nod at each other. He has to get to the school without looking at the sky. When he picks Tim up he has to help him with his homework and make him dinner and then put him to bed with a story. When Jeanne comes in he has to kiss her hello and serve her a plate of leftovers. Then he will sit back at his desk. Sit at his desk and know that the world has turned itself back to front and upside down and inside out. That the whole of everything has been inverted.

Kieran opens his eyes. The world shivers once but holds its shape. He gets up and leaves the imprint of his body on the sheets. He goes back to his desk and sits down. The top sheet of paper says:

Tea.

Hat.

Across the room the blue hat hangs on its peg, still and silent. Watching.

RONDO

Sarah Stanton

morning to night the mountains stumble
and their sheets are painted in ochre;
night to morning the thunder rumbles
and the green world slopes cleanly over.

Sunup, the little boy with a bell
and the sinking, shrinking showers;
I held it in my hands like a wind-up toy
and sent it purring over the world. Twinkle
wink, twinkle winking it went, a tinman decoy
in clicks and cogs while behind it the sky turned
pale; twinkle winking it went when I stripped down,
took my heart in my hands and fell onto it, all sawdust
and velvet but smiling, a short sunflower nested in a shell.

morning to night the mountains stumble
and their sheets are painted in ochre;
night to morning the thunder rumbles
and the green world slopes cleanly over.

It's the blue in the breach, the greasy feel
of June, the tune you let loose
with your feet and your gut when at last
you see the sun. It's the hot grass
after a storm, the worm under the earth,
the dog on its back with its paws
to the air like a rackety arfing hallelujah;
or perhaps it's you, fooling around
in the paddling pool as if the sky went on
forever and ever. Perhaps it's you

toddling up the lawn to show me a stone,
humming 'Hickory Dock' like a sutra
while we play at a slow game called noon.

morning to night the mountains stumble
and their sheets are painted in ochre;
night to morning the thunder rumbles
and the green world slopes cleanly over.

I've got mould on my soul, that awful grey-green grubbiness
that comes of living too long; but I've been scrubbing it
red-raw, going out when the street lights are dimmed
and rasping my fingers on the moon. Sometimes,
when the stars are out and I can see my skin
pink for the first time, I feel like a balloon
going up to heaven: a single breath
of helium blinking out of sight
while the night rolls on.

morning to night the mountains stumble
and their sheets are painted in ochre;
night to morning the thunder rumbles
and the green world slopes cleanly over.

THE ECHIDNA GAME

Peter Donaldson

'The echidna is the disgruntled grumblebum of the bush,' my mum used to tell me gleefully whenever the topic came up, and it came up far more often than it probably should have. We lived alone, me and her, for most of my childhood, on a little bush block on the edge of the desert in the Mallee. Dad had died when I was still too little to remember. That was the official line anyway, and I never questioned it too much. Still don't, and I'm pushing 40.

'No point dwellin' on the past boy,' mum would say, 'he's shuffled off and there ain't nothin' you or I can do to change that. Best to look at what's in front of you right now.' And there was always something in front of us out there, there always is for those with an eye for it. And mum sure as anything had an eye. Every morning after the jobs were done we went walking, and she could spot anything from a mile. I would always be daydreaming, then suddenly she would turn to me with that quick glance of her bright brown eyes, and I would know something was up. 'Follow me, boy,' she'd announce, grabbing my wrist with those wiry hands and dragging me off at a gallop to some far corner of the bush to see a red-cap robin, a baby emu, or a shingle-back. She got no end of joy out of invoking the overreactive tongue-hiss of the shingle-back. I can still hear her calling out, 'Ho ho ho, hey boy, check out this fiery little proud bugger,' as she poked in its general direction. Her whole thin body would convulse with laughter, and she would give me a bear-hug and ruffle my hair to celebrate. She was happiest around animals.

She was different when other people were around. They weren't often around, though. But she had to 'deal with 'em', as she put it, at the markets every Saturday. We grew pistachios, walnuts, almonds, and vegies at the block. On Saturdays we were always up at sparrow's fart picking and packing as much as we could into our little trailer, attached to mum's bike. It was always facing slightly downhill, so she could 'get the bugger rolling'. And roll we did, and bump and jump, the couple of hours it took her to pedal into town, with me bouncing around in back with the pumpkins and potatoes. Once I was old enough, I was in charge of 'customer relations' at the market. I learnt to say 'hello' and 'goodbye' and 'thank you ma'am' and give the correct change. Mum said my smile sold a million nuts and that she was better off in the background. And in the background she stayed, only emerging from the shadows of the stall tent to top up the walnut or almond crate occasionally. She looked different in town. Smaller. Older. Every now and then a customer and she would coincide 'out front' while she was topping up. I recall one day in particular when one of the customers said, 'How are you, Enid?' which confused me as I had no idea who that was. To my surprise, mum answered, 'Good,' with eyes downcast, and shuffled back to her usual spot. The same day, when returning to the stall after going to the toilet, I went past some women chatting and giggling under the old red gum by the amenities block. As I approached them I heard one of them say, 'Poor old nutty Enid, she'll never be the same. Thank heavens she has the boy to look after her though...' She trailed off as she caught sight of me and I pretended not to hear and hurried back to the stall.

Later on that afternoon when we were back at home, I decided to ask mum some questions. After we had finished unpacking, I said, 'Mum, why don't you talk to anybody in town?' She shot me a quick glance and let out a small sigh. 'Lets go for a walk, boy.' Mum did all her 'serious talking' on walks, and so we set off. That evening as the sun was dropping over the desert it gave out a deep peachy glow that weakened above us and reflected bright pink off the low clouds and big old pines behind us. We headed slowly toward the sun, weaving through the banksia and tea-tree, dead leaves crunching into the sand beneath our feet. The heath country here was all about chest height, with the odd cypress, stringybark or yellow gum silhouetted against the setting sun. Mum was walking in front, me behind – single file was the only way to get through these bits – and the brush scraped our sides as we squeezed through.

'The reason I don't talk to 'em...' mum began, 'is that that's all they do. Talk I mean. They all talk, an' they talk, but they don't talk about much that ain't pointless or mean. Times in the past I have talked with some of 'em I regretted it later. Can't keep their traps shut...' Mum's own talk was cut short at that point, as she heard a nearby rustle in the undergrowth. 'Hello!' she nearly shouted, and jumped over a broombush towards the source of the noise. 'Ha Ha! Just as I thought, it's the disgruntled grumblebum!' She reached back over and pulled me towards the scene of the action. She gave me one of her glances and I could see that the previous discussion, and her care-worn expression had been abandoned in an instant; her eyes shone and it was as if 20 years of worry had been shed from her face. The impatience of her explanation was child-like, 'Look! Look! See him burrow down into the sand! That's how he protects himself from us.' The echidna had indeed burrowed himself into a little hollow so that only his raised spikes were showing to the world above the earth. 'The silly thing is, we wouldn't have even heard him if he wasn't already trying to hide from us,' she continued, 'but then again they wouldn't have evolved with us humans in mind as predators. You know how long they been around? Since the dinosaurs. Can you imagine? Maybe that's why they're so bloody angry. Maybe the world has gone on an' left 'em behind. Most of the year they get around grumbling to themselves – they pretty much spend all their time alone. They walk around like long nosed bulldogs with sawn-off legs, getting annoyed at sticks that get in their way, annoyed there aint enough termites to eat. But sometime you see 'em in groups during the breeding season. And if you think their walkin' style is funny you should see 'em swim! Once I saw a whole train of 'em cross the river here. Wasn't that a sight! A troupe of spiky balloons bobbin' slowly across! But they got there eventually. They always do. Here, come here and sit down, sit there...'

I did so, positioning myself to the left of mum. The echidna had burrowed it's little half hole with its nose poking under an old grey log, below a banksia. We sat in a small semi-circle around it, wriggling our bums into the still-warm sand for comfort. 'This might take a while,' mum said, 'have you ever played the echidna game?' She looked overjoyed when I admitted I hadn't. 'It goes like this. We are now locked in battle with Mr Grumblebum here. He feels safe curled up in his little ball there, but he don't like it. It's uncomfy for him to have his legs, claws and nose all curled up under himself like that. He wants to unroll himself, but he has to learn to trust us first. Or maybe it's more like this; his uncomfiness needs to outweigh the risk he reckons we pose before he works up the guts to shuffle on. If he outlasts us he wins, if we outlast him we win!'

With the rules of the game established, there was nothing for it but to sit and wait. The stillness closed in quick. There was absolute quiet, broken only by a bit of goodnight bird-chatter. The sun fell below the desert skyline, and a heavy twilight wrapped everything with its magical silver. The rising moon was nearly full. The heat was climbing up out of the sand into the sky as the cold damp descended, slowly coating everything with it's earthy smell. As time wore on, the discomfort of the echidna became more obvious. His back wriggled and he muttered whilst adjusting, trying to find a more comfy position. 'They're pretty patient buggers,' mum whispered, 'I've waited over an hour before and still been pipped'. I looked over at mum. She was laying on her back now, looking up at the sky as the stars began to reveal themselves. The image of her laying there is still burned into me. She was looking over at the echidna occasionally, before chuckling quietly to herself and resuming her night-sky vigil. She looked more pale than ever in this light and the bared parts of her skin seemed to merge with the white desert sand. Her faded floral market frock was like a misplaced garden-bed, and as her coarse-straw hair fell in amongst the leaves and sticks, it seemed to draw some more of this matter into itself each time she moved. The grey half-light was kind to her face; it had a levelling effect. The brown spots on her face formed a lizard-scale web, and the moon bounced back out of her eyes. Suddenly, her eyes darted back to the echidna, 'Mr Grumblebum is on the move...' she whispered. Sure enough, the echidna, whilst still partly buried, had raised itself onto it's stumpy hind legs, and was stretching them as if to see if they still worked, and could be tested without any interference on our part. Having run this first test successfully, the echidna examined one front leg, then the next, stretching each for a seemingly set period of time. Finally, with abundant muttering and grumbling, the echidna shuffled off in visual protest against it's prior detainment. Mum grabbed my cold right hand with her warm left, and said with a secretive smile, 'It looks like we win tonight boy. Looks like we win.'

As the silver twilight began to fade, I fell in line behind mum as she headed back. With one arm holding the back of her dress, my spare hand was brushing over the serrated leaves of desert banksia. I could feel the dew beginning to form.

Etosha Milner

TAKE AWAY

Jeremy Johnson

Chip.

Chip. I see a chip. I want the chip. Give me the chip.

It's there, it's good, it's a chip, it's a Chip!

Quick. Get the Chip. I want the Chip. But he wants the Chip. And she wants the Chip. They all want the Chip, so quick, quick, get the Chip.

I look down from the tree. Claws gripping bark. I fall. I flap. Air. Feathers. I glide. I fall. I flap. I land on the metal statue.

Claws scratching. No grip. I stumble. I clutch on to metal. No grip. I fall. I flap. I land on stone. There's grip. I look.

Grass to the left. Grass to the right. Friends down there. Many of us. Crowding, hurrying, pecking. There's a Giant. He has a paper bag. He holds a blue pen, writes in a red book. From the bag he pulls the Chips. He eats one, I hear the crunch, the crunch of the Chip.

I flap. I fly. I land. So many feathers. My friends. I fight them. I peck a cousin. I claw my sister. The Giant sees. He smiles with his face. Giant face. He puts down the red book, the blue pen. Picks up another Chip. We stare. He laughs.

The Chip is golden. The Chip is steaming. It beckons us. I stab someone with my beak. The Giant sees. He stands. I watch. He hurls the Chip across the grass.

Jump, flap, fight, rush, grab, bite. Chip! Get the Chip! Got the Chip! I stumble, I fight. So many feathers. Someone claws my wing. I jump, I flap. I'm up, I'm flying and my friends drop away. The Chip hangs from my beak, flapping in the wind. It tears. I scream. Half falls. A mad rush of feathers below. I flap, I fly, up to the tree branches. I land, I stop, claws gripping bark.

I breathe. Thumping in my chest. I blink. Then, in ecstasy, I let the half Chip slide down my throat. It is golden, salty, steaming, crunchy, mushy, good. I breathe it inside.

The metal statue looks at me. The grass lawn and all my friends are below. I blink.

A good day.

PARIAN SAPPHO

Siobhan Hodge

Your hands and feet are
cut to fit, dotting
lines to mark the split
of rotting grammar
under sand. All lost,
the rhymes are lines pushed
to your lips and stuck:
sample selfish love.
We fret as half-known
symbols feed new strains,
do not eat what we
cannot name for sure.
Slips of gloss where rips
meat-deep are hushed and
sealed to strung-up bones,
we taste the resin's
cloying tones and wait:
the deadweight tug can
loose blunt agony,
fresh-dug from rubbish
pits, but second-hand
longing still only
feeds your curators.

NEWS

Susan Stanford

When the war started
I stopped
the paper, but
each time I hit the sack I turn on
the radio.
The news
bulletins hold me
in their predictable grip:
a lullaby (for adults)
repeated on the hour.
Helpless.
Helpless as a baby,
I can sleep.

The 2 a.m. fanfare.
A newsreader riffs
on the same theme:
missile, flood,
5,000, 50,000,
earthquake, suicide
bombing, hit and run,

disaster,
an aircrsha,
a murder,

the death of a child
whose mama
or papa
is being questioned
by the please!

Sleep, sleep.
At last, I can sleep.

These nightly rehearsals
are homeopathic
turn my foot into a hoof,
build a tank around my heart,
form my swaddling clothes
from a callous.

I once heard a newsreader
break into sobs.
It was newsworthy.
It would have cost him his job,
don't you think?

STUDY OF AN AFTERNOON IN A FLORIST

Amy Nicholls-Diver

Marie looked up at the brisk sound of the bell against the door. The woman that walked in the store was partly obscured by a spray of hydrangeas, so Marie shifted from the stool to see if she needed help. As she stood her dress swung around her dimpled knees. *Can I help you?* she asked. The woman peered up from the box of peonies. *Oh*, she said, and her forehead creased as she smiled. *I am looking for something for my sister. She's just had a baby.* The woman was beautiful, in the way that pretty people denied. Her hair was chin length and reddish brown like tiger lily pollen. Freckles made constellations on her high cheekbones. She wore no make-up, but her eyes were large, and spaced just that far apart to make a girl like Marie stare. *It's a girl,* she continued. Marie nodded, then cleared her throat and nodded again.

Of course! How wonderful, how absolutely wonderful! She smoothed her thick hair with both hands, a nervous habit acquired in high school. The woman looked up at Marie with her head tilted to the side. Marie blushed. She took a step back, nearly falling over the pails of fiery geraniums. The woman was both short and slim; Marie folded her arms across her breasts that appeared homely through the thin fabric of her dress.

It's my first niece, said the redhead. *I really don't know what to get; all this is beyond me.* The brief look of helplessness that flickered across her face surprised Marie.

It's not that hard, she replied, *I've just had more practice.* She looked about the oversized room. *You could go for one of the arrangements in the corner; they're always popular, especially if you're not sure what you're looking for in particular. Or I could help you put something together, if you want. Do you want to go with the traditional pink, or something different?* The woman's suit was grey; she didn't look like someone who wore a lot of pink.

I suppose pink is the done thing, isn't it? asked the woman. *Maybe I will just have a look at the arrangements.* She smiled awkwardly again. *I really have no idea; this is so different from what I do all day. What would a linguist know about floral arrangements?*

You're a linguist? Marie asked, letting the foreign sounding word uncurl from her tongue. *What is it that you do?*

I am still studying, postgraduate. It's the scientific study of language. Applying logic to all the chaos of interaction.

Oh, Marie said softly. *Is that hard?*

The woman in grey tugged at the hair behind her ear. *It's challenging, sure. But I like finding order in things. It's not for everyone though. I have to teach first years; they hate it. We had a class today on logic and the conditional. Inverse sentences. I've never seen two equations evoke so much anxiety.* She blinked heavily. *I'm sorry, I must be boring you. Prattling on about work to anyone who will listen. I'm Lucy.* She reached out and took Marie's hand. *Do you think pink is right?*

Pink? Marie asked. *Oh, yes. I'm sure it's perfect. I'll just... Why don't you look around, and I'll see how you're going in a few minutes?* She pulled her clammy hand from Lucy's and fled to the room behind the counter.

The back room was warmer than the shop floor. Marie ran the tap until the water was cool. She splashed her face and attempted to clear the dirt from under her short nails. The clock on the wall had been frozen at four for weeks, so she measured time by pacing up and down the floor that was littered with leaves and discarded scraps of ribbon.

When she emerged Lucy was standing with her back to the counter. She had taken off her jacket and her shirt was tailored to fit her slight frame. For the smallest moment Marie considered what it would be like to put her hands around that perfect waist. She flushed as Lucy turned and hoped her thoughts weren't written on her face.

I thought I would just take one of the arrangements, said Lucy and she offered Marie the basket she had chosen. *I didn't want to waste any of more of your time; I've rambled on already.*

It's no trouble! Marie cried. She smoothed her hair again. *But I am sure you're in a hurry to get somewhere.*

Not especially. Lucy bit the inside of her bottom lip. *I feed the cat in the morning, and I haven't heard what time they want visitors. I'm sure they're all focussed on the little one; it's dreadfully nice.* She shifted the jacket from one arm to the other and pushed up the sleeves of her shirt. Her hair caught the evening sun that fell though the store's bay window and the loose wisps glistened gold.

They stood in silence again, each with lungs full of hesitation. Marie looked down at the arrangement and tweaked a few of the leaves. She was about to speak when Lucy's phone rang. Lucy let out a laugh that was more of a gasp. Smiling apologetically, she answered and walked to the furthest corner of the room from the counter.

Marie picked up the book she had abandoned earlier, but before she finished a page, her eyes wandered back to Lucy. She looked concerned and from across the room Marie could see the skin above her collarbones turn a vivid red. She wondered if it was an ex-lover. Not wanting to appear nosey, she sat back on the stool and held the book close to her face.

A few moments later, Lucy rushed back towards the register. Her eyes were wild with tears. She picked up her bag from the floor.

I have to go. She looked around, as though seeing the room for the first time. *I'm so sorry. I don't even ... Family stuff. I ...* She rubbed her brow with her free hand.

Marie moved around the counter but as she reached out her hand Lucy pulled away. *I'm sorry*, Lucy said again. Phone in hand, she left.

Just as it ushered her arrival, the bell marked her departure. The store was empty; Marie swung the sign in the window to 'Closed'.

THE DONKEY DECIDES

Samuel Robertson

A boy, a voice, a sea, a sky.

A choice.

Boy stands along the horizontal line dividing Sea and Sky.

It begins.

Voice: You must choose between Sea and Sky.

Boy: Why?

Voice: You cannot have both.

Boy: Why?

Voice: When you gain something, you lose something.

Boy: That hardly seems fair.

Voice: Life isn't fair.

Boy: No.

Voice: So you must decide.

Boy: First things first, I will assemble the facts.

Voice: Very well.

Boy: What will happen to the animals?

Voice: What do you mean?

Boy: Birds cannot swim and whales cannot fly.

Voice: No, they cannot.

Boy: So, what happens to them?

Voice: I do not know.

Boy: You expect me to decide between Sea and Sky without knowing what will happen to birds that cannot swim and whales that cannot fly?

Voice: The facts are unavailable.

Boy: It is impossible to make a reasoned judgment without the facts.

Voice: Make the impossible possible.

Boy: It is logically impossible to make the impossible possible.

Voice: Whatever the case, you must decide.

[Boy, incredulous]

Boy: Based on what!?

Voice: Any number of things.

Boy: Such as?

Voice: A coin-toss.

Boy: Too arbitrary.

Voice: A double-headed coin.

Boy: How do I choose which to assign heads – Sea or Sky?

Voice: That is for you to decide.

[Terse silence]

Boy: What do you suggest?

Voice: Faith.

Boy: Faith is an arms-reach answer.

Voice: It is a way of moving forward.

Boy: Forward to ignorance.

Voice: Forward to progress.

Boy: Without reason we are without progress.

Voice: You're not making much progress with all these reasonable questions.

Boy: That is because you will not answer!

Voice: That is because there is no answer.

[They fall silent]

Boy: What if I do not choose?

Voice: Then you have chosen.

Boy: Chosen what?

Voice: Indecision is a decision.

Boy: Indecision is a decision not to decide?

Voice: Yes.

Boy: Now I have a headache.

[Boy rubs his head]

Voice: Have you heard the story of the donkey?

Boy: The one with the palm branches and the preacher?

Voice: No.

Boy: Then I do not know the story.

Voice: A thirsty, hungry donkey is standing in the middle of two identical tables with hay and water. It is starving and dehydrated.

Boy: And?

Voice: The donkey cannot choose between the tables and dies.

Boy: Why did the donkey not decide?

Voice: There was no reason for the donkey to choose one table over the other.

Boy: The donkey was irrational.

Voice: The donkey was perfectly rational.

Boy: The donkey was stupid.

Voice: If you say so.

Boy stands along the horizontal line dividing Sea and Sky and continues asking questions. It goes like this for many days, many months, many years.

Until ...

Boy: I have come to a decision.

Voice: What have you chosen?

Boy: It's the only sensible decision.

Voice: What is your decision?

Boy: The only reasonable conclusion.

Voice: What is it?

Boy: Without all the facts I have no other choice.

Voice: What do you decide?

[Boy, forceful]

Boy: I choose neither!

[Voice is silent]

Boy: Did you hear me?

[Boy, fearful]

Boy: I choose neither.

[Voice is gone]

[Sea is gone]

[Sky is gone]

It was the day that the master purchased the hall mirror that Jacques, spying his reflection, first came to terms with his troubling subjectivity.

Jacques
Elizabeth Tan

VERGE CONTRIBUTORS

Amber Beilharz has poetry, nonfiction and fiction in *Voiceworks Magazine*. Her fiction appears in *antiTHESIS* and *Hunger Mountain* and poetry within *dotdotdash*, *Fragmented* and *Verandah*. She is currently a poetry editor at *Voiceworks Magazine* and blogs at www.metremaids.com. Her twitter handle is @velvetbrownfox.

Ineke Dane was born on the east coast of Australia. She sailed to Berlin at the end of 2011 after completing a law degree to pursue photography and eat apples – www.inekedane.com.

Peter Dawncy has a Bachelor of Arts with majors in English and Philosophy from Monash University and this year is commencing his PhD in creative writing. Peter has had poetry published in *Southerly*, *Mascara Literary Review*, *Islet*, *LINQ*, *Voiceworks* and in previous editions of *Verge*. Email: peter.dawncy@gmail.com.

Peter Donaldson: born in Temora and previously a plant-grower, Peter Donaldson is currently studying at Monash University, focusing on creative writing, philosophy and psychology. He divides his time between Melbourne and Dimboola. Contact: pdonaldson@hotmail.com.

Matt Hetherington: musician, writer, and sook living in Thornbury. Has a decent heater. His most recent poetry collection is "Eye to Eye" (*PRECIOUS PRESS*, 2012), and in 2006, he was co-editor of "Straight from the Tank", a performance-documentary film featuring over 60 poetry performances in Melbourne from 2003-2005.

Siobhan Hodge is a doctoral candidate at the University of Western Australia from the discipline of English, studying Sappho's poetry and its translation. She divides her time between Australia and Hong Kong, and writes poetry, fiction and essays. She can be contacted at kunoichi666@gmail.com.

Jeremy Johnson is a Creative Writing student at RMIT. He's also a teacher of karate-do and a collector of fedora hats, but it's the writing that makes him fly. You should see him dancing on a notepad. His heart is made of train-smoke and mistakes. Jeremy can be found at: http://excalamus.com/tagged/Jeremy-Johnson.

Jenny Luong is a law and arts student at Monash, but hopefully for not much longer.

Emily McNamara is a graduate of both Brighton Bay Art, Design & Photography and Monash University (Bachelor of Design). She now works full time in the big bad advertising world and enjoys striped clothing, textile design, jogging and sparkly things. You can say hello to her at: ejmcnamara@hotmail.com

Etosha Milner is a student of environmental engineering that takes the occasional pleasure in drawing. Eventually his drawing started to creep into his nights of study and as various concepts have evolved he has endeavoured to capture them in his work. You can check out his page at www.facebook.com/AWellDressedWolf.

Bruce Mutard is the author 4 graphic novels: *The Sacrifice* (Allen & Unwin, 2008), *The Silence* (Allen & Unwin, 2009), *A Mind of Love* (Black House Comics, 2011), *The Bunker* (Image Comics, 2003) and one collection of short stories: *Stripshow* (Milk Shadow Books, 2012). He also has had stories in *Overland, Meanjin, The Australian Book Review* among others. You can find him at: www.brucemutard.com.

Amy Nicholls-Diver is completing her Honours thesis on the work of Marilyn Hacker. She has been published twice previously in *Verge*, and has a poem in the most recent edition of *lip* (Issue 21). The completion of her novella (three years in the making) is her next literary goal.

Catherine Noske is working to complete her doctorate in Creative Writing at Monash University. She was a co-editor of both *Verge 2011: The Unknowable* and *Verge 2007*, and has been published in it twice. She was recognized as part of the Sir John Monash Medal (2008) for her achievements in creative writing. Her short stories have been twice awarded the Elyne Mitchell Prize for Rural Women Writers.

Vidya Rajan is a Law/Arts (honours) student at the University of Western Australia. Her writing interests lie in poetry, short fiction and theatre, but too often emerge in the well oiled facebook update. She can be contacted at:rajan.s.vidya@gmail.com.

Samuel Robertson was a student editor of the *Verge* anthology in 2010. This year he is on the other side of the divide. He is currently completing a degree in Arts/Commerce at Monash University.

Sue Stanford is currently completing her PhD on the haiku poet Sugita Hisajo at Monash in Japanese Studies. She edited the MPU national anthology of tea, wine and coffee poetry, *The Attitude of Cups* in 2011. Two of her own collections of poetry, 'Opal' and 'The Neon City', have been published since 2006.

Sarah Stanton is a native Western Australian working in Beijing as a freelance translator and editor specialising in Chinese literature. She has been published in a variety of magazines, including *Cha*, *Voiceworks*, *Hunger Mountain*, and *dotdotdash*, and was recently shortlisted for the James White Award. She blogs at http://www.theduckopera.com.

Elizabeth Tan is undertaking a Creative Writing PhD at Curtin University in Perth. Her work has appeared in *dotdotdash*, *Voiceworks* and *Sitelines*, and also in the anthologies *Nth Degree* and *Epilogue*. She blogs at et-maispourquoi.blogspot.com.

Stephanie Yap is a Melbourne based designer and recent Monash graduate. She enjoys exploring and creating work that is experimental, handmade, and also has a sense of humour. You can find more of her work at: www.stephanieyap.com.

ACKNOWLEDGEMENTS

This edition of Verge is indebted to a number of people in its realisation. Firstly, to Dr Ali Alizadeh for his enthusiasm, problem-solving and calm resolve in helping us to combat the bumps along the way. To Associate Professor Chandani Lokuge, who has been the force behind Verge for the past seven years, for willingly entrusting the publication to us this year with her full confidence. We are extremely grateful to the School of English, Communications and Performance Studies, especially Jodie Wood and Professor Sue Kossew, and the Centre for Postcolonial Writing at Monash for their continued support of Verge. We would also like to thank the Dean of Arts, Professor Raelene Frances, and the Faculty of Arts for making both this publication and its launch possible.

We would also like to thank our dedicated referees, whose feedback and support have afforded us a higher quality of work throughout the publication: Peter Blegvad, Matt Hall, Professor Trevor Harris, Dr John Hawke, Anna Lea, Kent MacCarter, Professor Lyn McCredden, Professor Stephen Muecke, Associate Professor Kate Rigby, Dr Chris Worth, Professor Van Ikin, Dr Venero Armanno, Dr Bronwyn Lea, Jill Jones and Caroline McKinnon.

We owe many a thankyou to "the Davids": David Hall and David Muller for their speed, attention to detail and professionalism within the proofreading process; and so too to the team at Monash University Press, in particular Nathan Hollier and Jo Mullins, who have published Verge for the second consecutive year, and have provided us with a great deal of assistance in the process.

Our launch at the Melbourne Writers' Festival is a source of great pride, and we would like to thank the team at the Festival for their support and assistance in bringing this to fruition again in 2012. Thanks should also go to The Grumpy Swimmer Bookstore in Elwood for their contribution to our fiction prize, and equally to Collected Works Bookshop in Melbourne for our poetry prize. These relationships that Verge holds with the wider literary community are of great value, and we appreciate them immensely.

Most of all, to our contributors whose work fills these pages- a very big heartfelt thank you from us both. You have made working on Verge this year such an exciting and rewarding experience, and your willingness to work with us every step of the way has not gone unnoticed. Thank you too, to all of those who submitted their work for consideration.

We very much hope that in reading this year's edition of Verge, you will enjoy it as much as we did putting it together.

Samantha Clifford and Rosalind McFarlane, Editors, *Verge 2012*